Captain and Matey Set Sail

story by Daniel Laurence

pictures by Claudio Muñoz

HarperCollinsPublishers

For my celebrity heroes,
treasures on the stormy sea of humanity:
Jimmy Carter and Elton John
—D.L.

To Louie
—C.M.

HarperCollins®, ▙®, and I Can Read Book®
are trademarks of HarperCollins Publishers Inc.

Captain and Matey Set Sail
Text copyright © 2001 by Daniel Laurence Andersen
Illustrations copyright © 2001 by Claudio Muñoz
Printed in the U.S.A. All rights reserved.
www.harperchildrens.com

Library of Congress Cataloging-in-Publication Data
Laurence, Daniel.
  Captain and Matey set sail / by Daniel Laurence ; pictures by Claudio Muñoz.
    p.   cm.
  Summary: Despite their frequent disagreements, two pirates share many
adventures.
  ISBN 0-06-028956-2 — ISBN 0-06-028957-0 (lib. bdg.)
  [1. Pirates—Fiction.]   I. Muñoz, Claudio, ill.   II. Title.   III. Series.
PZ7.L372775 Cap   2001   00-035008
[E]—dc21

1 2 3 4 5 6 7 8 9 10
❖
First Edition

Contents

On the warm seas sailed a ship.

On the ship lived two pirates.

Their names were Captain and Matey.

Captain was the captain of the ship.

Matey was first mate.

The Parrot's Name

One day Captain said,

"Look at our ship, Matey.

It is a good pirate ship."

"With a good

pirate plank,"

Matey added.

"Just look at our strong sails and our sturdy wheel," said Captain. "We have everything we need to be good pirates."

"Yes," said Matey, "everything except a parrot."

So the pirates . . .

8

chips   chops

pens   pins

pets pats

got a parrot.

"Let's call her Polly,"
said Captain.

"Forget it," said Matey.

"Every pirate's parrot
is called Polly."

The parrot said, "Squawk."

"I think we should call her Spot,"

said Matey.

"SPOT! That's a dog's name.

Besides, she doesn't have any spots,"

said Captain.

The parrot said, "Squawk,"

a little louder.

"What about Mildred?" said Captain.

"It is such a lovely name."

"That is your mother's name,

and she doesn't like birds,"

said Matey.

The parrot looked at Matey
and said, "Squawk," very loudly.
She looked at Captain
and said, "Squawk," even louder.

13

"What about Greenie?" asked Captain.

"She is mostly green."

"Or Princess?" asked Matey.

"We will

treat her like a princess!"

"Feathers?" asked Captain.

"Or Beakers?"

asked Matey.

Suddenly, the parrot
flew around and around,
screeching, "Squawk,
squawk, SQUAWK!"

"Captain," said Matey,

"I think the parrot

is trying to tell us something."

"Is your name Squawk?"

Captain asked the parrot.

The parrot flew

to Captain's shoulder.

Very, very softly

she said, "Squawk."

16

From then on,

the parrot was called Squawk.

After all, Squawk was her name.

A Pirate Song

Thursday was deck-swabbing day.

Captain swabbed one end of the deck.

Matey swabbed the other end.

Matey sang softly,

"Row, row, row your boat

gently down the stream."

Captain sang,

"Yo-ho-ho and a bottle of rum."

He did not sing softly.

The harder Captain swabbed,

the louder he sang.

"Yo-ho-ho and a bottle of rum!"

"I hate that song,"

Matey told Squawk.

"Captain sings so loud

even the sharks can hear."

So, Matey sang louder.

"Row, row, row your boat

gently down the stream!"

"Boy, I hate that song,"

Captain said to himself.

So, Captain sang louder, too.

Both pirates sang louder and louder,

and both pirates grew

madder and madder.

Captain stopped swabbing.

He marched up to Matey.

"Matey," he said,

"I hate that song.

It is not a pirate song.

First, this is not a stream.

It is the sea.

Also, we are on a ship,

not a boat.

Lastly, pirates don't do
anything gently."

Matey said, "True, this is a ship

and not a boat,

and we are on the sea,

not a stream.

But, *I* am a pirate,

and *I* do things gently!

Anyway, I hate *your* song."

"Just why is that?" asked Captain.

"First," said Matey,

"'yo-ho-ho' means nothing,

and you do not even like rum.

I saw you drink rum one time

and it made you sick."

"It is true I don't like rum,"

said Captain,

"but I do like to sing 'yo-ho-ho.'

Singing 'yo-ho-ho' makes me feel

like a pirate."

"Well, just stop singing it

for a little while," said Matey.

"My ears need a rest."

"I won't," said Captain. "You stop."

"No, you!" said Matey.

"You!" shouted Captain.

"YOU!" yelled Matey.

"Yo-ho-ho, gently on the sea,

yo-ho-ho, gently on the sea,"

squawked Squawk.

"What a wonderful idea!"

said Matey.

"Yes," said Captain,

"I like the sound of that."

So, Captain and Matey

sat down together

and wrote a new song.

There were no streams

or rum in it,

but it had plenty of yo-ho-ho's

and gently's,

and they both liked it.

"It is very pirate-like," said Captain.

"Yet gentle," added Matey.

Captain and Matey swabbed

and sang together,

and every time the pirates sang,

Squawk squawked in.

The Visitor

"Look, Captain," said Matey,

"there is a pirate in the water."

The pirate swam to the ship

and called to Captain,

"Sir, I fell off my ship.

Will you give me a ride to shore?"

"We'd be happy to," said Captain.

"Matey, throw a rope

to our visitor."

The visitor climbed on board.

He was big and scruffy and strong.

"Now, that's a pirate,"

said Matey.

Captain said, "I had better climb up

to the crow's nest to see

if there are any other pirates

floating about."

"I would be happy to do that

for you, sir," said the visitor.

He started climbing.

"Wow!" said Matey.

"Look at how fast he is climbing!

Now, that's a pirate!"

Captain frowned.

Near dinnertime Captain said,

"We only have two fish.

I will catch another

for our visitor."

"I would be happy to do that

for you, sir," said the visitor.

The visitor dived into the sea

and came up

with a fish in his bare hands.

"Wow," said Matey,

"fishing with bare hands.

Now, that's a pirate!"

Captain rolled his eyes.

"Big deal," he muttered.

After dinner,

Matey said to the visitor,

"Tomorrow we will reach land.

What will you do then?"

The visitor said, "I was thinking

of getting another tattoo."

"Another tattoo?" asked Matey.

"Do you have one now?"

"I have many," said the visitor.

The visitor had tattoos on his back.

He had tattoos on his legs and chest,

and he had tattoos on his arms.

Matey said, "Now, that's a—"

"Yes," roared Captain,

"he is quite a pirate!

He is big and scruffy.

He can climb the ropes fast.

He can catch fish in his bare hands,

and he has many tattoos!

But, I am the captain," he shouted,

"and I say it has been a long day

and we should all go to bed!"

"Not yet, Captain," said Matey.

"It is our visitor's last night here.

We must have a party. Let's dance!"

"No," said Captain. "I am tired

and I am going to bed."

"It is all right, sir.

I do not know how to dance

anyway," said the visitor.

"You don't know how to dance?"

asked Captain.

"All real pirates must know

how to dance, but do not worry.

I will show you how."

Captain danced and danced.

Matey and Squawk danced, too.

The visitor just watched.

When they reached shore,

the visitor left.

"Wow," said Matey.

"Now, there goes a pirate!"

"Maybe," said Captain,

"but it's too bad

he's not much of a dancer!"

Treasure

"It was nice of the visitor

to give us his treasure map,"

said Matey.

"I hope the treasure is jewels.

With jewels we can make crowns.

They will sparkle in the sun."

"We will not make crowns,"

said Captain.

"Whoever heard of such a thing!

We will sell the jewels

and buy a bigger ship."

"But I have always wanted a crown,"

said Matey.

"We will get a bigger ship!"

said Captain.

"Crowns!" said Matey.

"A bigger ship!" roared Captain.

"Well, since we cannot agree,

we will just have to disagree,"

said Matey.

"It will probably not be jewels
anyway," said Captain.

"I think it will be gold coins."

"That would be exciting,"
said Matey.

"We could buy a little house
by the sea, with a garden,

52

and a horse and a—"

"Oh, no," said Captain.

"We will buy new ropes and a cannon.

We are staying on the sea.

We are pirates!"

"Very well," said Matey,

"we will have to disagree again."

Captain became angry.

"No, Matey. Let's not disagree,

let's agree. Let's agree that

we will split the treasure.

I will take half.

You will take half.

I can buy a bigger ship

and you can make crowns

in your new house by the sea."

"Agreed," said Matey.

Captain shoveled,

and as he shoveled, he thought.

He thought about sailing

a big ship without Matey.

He felt sad.

Matey thought, too.

He thought about living

in a little house without Captain.

He felt sad.

Captain and Matey dug and dug

and felt sadder and sadder.

Finally, they hit something.

It was a treasure chest.

They took the chest out of the hole.

"Well," said Captain, "here it is."

"Yes, here it is," said Matey.

They stood there.

They did not open the chest.

"My big ship will seem very little

without you," said Captain.

"And my little house

will seem large and empty

without you," said Matey.

59

Captain opened the chest.

He peered into it and smiled.

He took out one gold coin

and one emerald.

He gave the emerald to Matey.

"Is that it?" asked Matey.

"Yes," said Captain.

"Oh, thank goodness," said Matey.

"I do not need a house anyway."

"And I," said Captain,

"do not need a bigger ship.

Besides, we have this great chest."

"Yes," said Matey,

"and it will be lovely

to keep dishes and napkins in."

"Dishes and napkins!" said Captain.

"Don't you mean daggers and swords?"

"No, I mean dishes and napkins!"

said Matey.

"Daggers and swords!" said Captain.

"DISHES AND NAPKINS!"

shouted Matey.

Matey and Captain argued.

They argued all the way

back to the ship.

They walked onto the ship,
still arguing.

The gold coin came with them.

The emerald came with them.

BUT the chest stayed on shore.